KINDERGARTEN, HERE I COME!

by D. J. Steinberg

illustrated by Mark Chambers

Grosset & Dunlap
An Imprint of Penguin Group (USA) Inc.

To Daphne, who brings magic to her classroom,
and special thanks to the incomparable Jane O'Connor
for her support and inspiration—DJS

For Kirsten, many thanks for your continued work across the pond—MC

GROSSET & DUNLAP
Published by the Penguin Group
Penguin Group (USA) Inc., 375 Hudson Street, New York, New York 10014, USA
Penguin Group (Canada), 90 Eglinton Avenue East, Suite 700, Toronto,
Ontario M4P 2Y3, Canada (a division of Pearson Penguin Canada Inc.)
Penguin Books Ltd., 80 Strand, London WC2R 0RL, England
Penguin Group Ireland, 25 St. Stephen's Green, Dublin 2, Ireland
(a division of Penguin Books Ltd.)
Penguin Group (Australia), 250 Camberwell Road, Camberwell, Victoria 3124, Australia
(a division of Pearson Australia Group Pty. Ltd.)
Penguin Books India Pvt. Ltd., 11 Community Centre, Panchsheel Park, New Delhi—110 017, India
Penguin Group (NZ), 67 Apollo Drive, Rosedale, Auckland 0632, New Zealand
(a division of Pearson New Zealand Ltd.)
Penguin Books (South Africa) (Pty.) Ltd., 24 Sturdee Avenue,
Rosebank, Johannesburg 2196, South Africa

Penguin Books Ltd., Registered Offices: 80 Strand, London WC2R 0RL, England

Text copyright © 2012 by David Steinberg. Illustrations copyright © 2012 by Penguin Group (USA) Inc. All rights reserved.
Published by Grosset & Dunlap, a division of Penguin Young Readers Group, 345 Hudson Street, New York, New York 10014.
GROSSET & DUNLAP is a trademark of Penguin Group (USA) Inc. Printed in the U.S.A.

Library of Congress Control Number: 2011043239

ISBN 978-0-448-45624-9 (pbk)
ISBN 978-0-448-46102-1 (hc)

20 19 18 17 16 15 14
10 9 8 7 6 5 4 3

Kindergarten, Here I Come!

Kindergarten, here I come . . .
I'm checking off the list
of everything I need for school.
Let's see . . . what have I missed?

Backpack . . . check. ✔
Glue stick . . . check. ✔
A labeled cubby box. ✔
Extra pair of underwear. ✔
Extra pair of socks. ✔
Crayons . . . check. ✔
Scissors . . . check. ✔
Mom says I'm all set.

But wait—there are
tons of other stuff
I'd better not forget!
My cuddle bear,
my magic wand,
my superhero cape,
two flashlights, and a tool set,
in case I must escape.

4

Huh? Mom says to put those things
back where I took them from.
She says that I won't need that stuff.
She promised school won't be too rough.
I hope she's right . . .
I really do 'cause . . .

kindergarten, here I come!

My Teacher

My teacher did a magic trick
the minute that I came.
I don't know how, but—**Presto! Poof!**—
she somehow knew my name!

Then—**Bam!**—she figured out I'm nice
and that I'm really smart.
And just like that she seemed to know
how good I am at art!

I think she used some magic spells
to make the whole day fun.
Of all the teachers in the world,
I'm glad that she's **my** one!

Crisscross Applesauce

Crisscross applesauce, that's the way we sit.
Not feet-out sauerkraut.
Not cottage cheese on your knees.
Not bottoms-up coffee cup.
Not blueberry jelly on your belly.
But crisscross applesauce, that's the way we sit!

Once Upon a Story Time

Goblins,
bunnies,
kings and queens,
cats in hats,
and magic beans.
Once upon a far away . . .
which book will we read today?

Yellow Lunch Box

I love you, yellow lunch box.
Click! I open you to see
what treasures lie inside today—
what did Mom pack for me?
Aha! So there you are—
below those good things I should eat.
I found you, chocolate cupcake—
you're my favorite part, the treat!

Missing Tooth

I was munching on my apple
when suddenly—*CRUNCH!*
My tongue felt something missing,
and I had a little hunch.
Out came a tiny pebble,
all shiny, smooth, and white.
**"HEY, LOOK! THE TOOTH FAIRY'S
COMING TO MY HOUSE TONIGHT!"**

Recess

I'm a fireman
to the rescue!
Down the pole I slide.
Look now—
I'm a monkey
swinging side to side.
I'm a climber,
up the mountain.
I'm queen of this whole town!
Check me out—
I'm a bat
hanging upside down!
Watch me creep
across this beam—
I'm a sneaky, thief raccoon.
I'm the pilot
of a rocket ship
zooming to the moon!
In only half an hour,
we are all these things and
more—
Till recess time is over
and we head back in the door!

Counting Craze!

There are 22 children here in Room 109,
a guinea pig, 3 goldfish, and 1 cuddle bear—mine!
There's 1 really nice teacher with 8 buttons on her dress
and 1 billion purple polka dots (more or less).
There are 39 crayons that fell out of the box,
53 cars, and 87 blocks.
24 food cans in our make-believe shop . . .
Oh, HELP!
I've learned how to count.
Now I just can't stop!

No Nap Rap

I'm not tired.
I'm not sleepy.
I'm wide-awake, you see!
It's daytime.
It's my playtime.
You say nap time? Not for me!

I'll lie flat
upon the mat,
but I'm not counting sheep!
You can snooze,
but I refuse.
Oh no, I WILL NOT GO TO . . .
ZZZZZZZZZZZZZZZZZZZ

Field Trip

Hooray! Hooray! A field trip day!
Adventure's in the air!
Driver, driver, please don't stop
until you get us there!

We squeal and hoot, we screech and roar
and stomp the whole way through,
just like a bunch of animals
until we reach the zoo!

Best Friends

Heather was my *best* friend
this morning on the *bus*,
but she talked so much to Shauna
that I made my *best friend* Gus.

But Gus said he was Noah's friend
and wouldn't take it back—
so I had to go and trade him
for a better best friend, Zack.

Zack wouldn't share
the box of *blocks*,
so what else could I do?
At lunchtime, I sat right down *beside*
my newest best friend, Sue.

Then Sue ate half my cupcake.
I didn't say she could!
In Art, I was all by myself—
I was done with friends for good!

Then someone came and asked me,
"Can we paint together?"

George

I have a kindergarten friend who isn't very big.
I'm talking 'bout George Washington, our classroom guinea pig.
I always stop to talk to him about the stuff we like.
I tell him what's on TV and how to ride a bike.
I'm teaching him his ABCs and how to draw a heart.
He always pays attention—that George is clearly very smart!

100th Day of School

I brought 100 marbles
inside my plastic cup.
Zack brought 100 chocolate chips
(till someone ate them up).

Nina's 100 toothpicks
all came inside one box.
Alia brought a picture
of her 100 chicken pox.
I used to think 100
was a lot when I was small,
but now that it's the 100th day,
I am old enough to say—
100 isn't all that many, many days at all!

Show-and-Tell

Today's my turn for show-and-tell,
but somehow I forgot!
I could have brought in cuddle bear
or else my new robot.
I could have brought my snow globe
or my cool vacation hat.
I could have brought my goldfish—
except I didn't think of that.
So now my hands are empty
and my teacher's calling me!
But hang on! I *see* something
staring right in front of me.

Quick! I draw two dots
on my finger while I stand.
Then I make my thumb into a mouth—
"Hi, class. Please meet my HAND!"

Line Leaders

"Line-up time!"
It's a race!
Everybody wants first place!
But I go s l o w l y . . .
I don't run . . .
'cause I'm the line leader.
I was picked the line leader!
So make way, kids,
for number one!

Growing Seeds

We planted seeds in paper cups
and put them on the sill.
We watered them
and watched . . .
and watched . . .
and watched those cups until . . .

I peeked today and—check it out—
a little baby seedling sprout!

Growing Me

What happened to my favorite pants?
The ones that used to fit.
Now they come up to my knees
when I try to sit.
My toes can't wiggle in my shoes
the way they used to do.
I think somebody shrunk my clothes.
Or could it be I grew?

Last Day

I hugged my teacher—
"Please don't cry!"
And she said, "Beg your pardon?"
I said, "We're going to first grade,
but you're stuck in Kindergarten!"